CHAPTER 1

A Fancy Coffin

Hello! My name is Elizabeth Wakefield. I am seven years old. I have a sister and a brother. My sister's name is Jessica. Jessica and I are twins—*identical* twins. That means we look exactly like each other. We have blue-green eyes and long blond hair.

My brother's name is Steven. He's two years older than Jessica and me. He thinks he's special, just because he was born first! He's a big pain.

Jessica and Steven and I live in Sweet Valley with our mom and dad.

We go to Sweet Valley Elementary School. Jessica and I are in second grade. Our teacher is Mrs. Otis. We're the only twins in our whole school.

Lots of people figure that Jessica and I will act like each other just because we *look* like each other. But they're always surprised! Jessica acts like Jessica, and I act like me!

I love school. I even like doing homework and going to the library. You can find out lots of interesting stuff at the library—even some *spooky* stuff. That's the most fun of all.

Jessica likes school too. But she hates homework, and she would rather play with her dolls than read. She only goes to the library when Mom or Dad or Mrs. Otis makes her. That's why she wasn't with Andy Franklin and me the day we read all about the Curse of the Pharaohs.

Sullivan

A Mummy's Curse . . .

"The pharaoh's tomb is cursed," Andy announced. "Anyone who interrupts the mummy's sleep dies."

"Remember how Henry said they couldn't get Egyptians to work on the dig?" I asked.

The other kids all nodded.

"Well, that was because they were afraid they'd die!" Andy said. Behind his glasses, his eyes were round.

"I think *Henry* is cursed," Jessica said. "He was there when they opened King Ramses' tomb. And then he got sick and had to leave our class."

"That's true," Andy said.

I was starting to feel a little worried about the trip to the Egyptian exhibit. I hoped King Ramses the Thirteenth wouldn't be angry with us for going to the museum.

But what if he *was*?

Bantam Books in the SWEET VALLEY KIDS series

#1	SURPRISE! SURPRISE!	#30	JESSICA'S UNBURIED TREASURE
#2	RUNAWAY HAMSTER	#31	ELIZABETH AND JESSICA RUN AWAY
#3	THE TWINS' MYSTERY TEACHER	#32	LEFT BACK!
#4	ELIZABETH'S VALENTINE	#33	CAROLINE'S HALLOWEEN SPELL
#5	JESSICA'S CAT TRICK	#34	THE BEST THANKSGIVING EVER
#6	LILA'S SECRET	#35	ELIZABETH'S BROKEN ARM
#7	JESSICA'S BIG MISTAKE	#36	ELIZABETH'S VIDEO FEVER
#8	JESSICA'S ZOO ADVENTURE	#37	THE BIG RACE
#9	ELIZABETH'S SUPER-SELLING LEMONADE	#38	GOOD-BYE, EVA?
#10	THE TWINS AND THE WILD WEST	#39	ELLEN IS HOME ALONE
#11	CRYBABY LOIS	#40	ROBIN IN THE MIDDLE
#12	SWEET VALLEY TRICK OR TREAT	#41	THE MISSING TEA SET
#13	STARRING WINSTON EGBERT	#42	JESSICA'S MONSTER NIGHTMARE
#14	JESSICA THE BABY-SITTER	#43	JESSICA GETS SPOOKED
#15	FEARLESS ELIZABETH	#44	THE TWINS' BIG POW-WOW
#16	JESSICA THE TV STAR	#45	ELIZABETH'S PIANO LESSONS
#17	CAROLINE'S MYSTERY DOLLS	#46	GET THE TEACHER!
#18	BOSSY STEVEN	#47	ELIZABETH THE TATTLETALE
#19	JESSICA AND THE JUMBO FISH	#48	LILA'S APRIL FOOL
#20	THE TWINS GO TO THE HOSPITAL	#49	JESSICA'S MERMAID
#21	JESSICA AND THE SPELLING-BEE SURPRISE	#50	STEVEN'S TWIN
#22	SWEET VALLEY SLUMBER PARTY	#51	LOIS AND THE SLEEPOVER
#23	LILA'S HAUNTED HOUSE PARTY	#52	JULIE THE KARATE KID
#24	COUSIN KELLY'S FAMILY SECRET	#53	THE MAGIC PUPPETS
#25	LEFT-OUT ELIZABETH	#54	STAR OF THE PARADE
#26	JESSICA'S SNOBBY CLUB	#55	THE JESSICA AND ELIZABETH SHOW
#27	THE SWEET VALLEY CLEANUP TEAM	#56	JESSICA PLAYS CUPID
#28	ELIZABETH MEETS HER HERO	#57	NO GIRLS ALLOWED
#29	ANDY AND THE ALIEN	#58	LILA'S BIRTHDAY BASH
		#59	JESSICA + JESSICA = TROUBLE

SWEET VALLEY KIDS SUPER SNOOPER EDITIONS
#1	THE CASE OF THE SECRET SANTA
#2	THE CASE OF THE MAGIC CHRISTMAS BELL
#3	THE CASE OF THE HAUNTED CAMP
#4	THE CASE OF THE CHRISTMAS THIEF
#5	THE CASE OF THE HIDDEN TREASURE
#6	THE CASE OF THE MILLION-DOLLAR DIAMONDS
#7	THE CASE OF THE ALIEN PRINCESS

SWEET VALLEY KIDS SUPER SPECIAL EDITIONS
#1	TRAPPED IN TOYLAND
#2	THE EASTER BUNNY BATTLE

SWEET VALLEY KIDS HAIR RAISER EDITIONS
A CURSE ON ELIZABETH

SWEET VALLEY KIDS

A CURSE ON ELIZABETH

Written by
Molly Mia Stewart

Created by
FRANCINE PASCAL

Illustrated by
Ying-Hwa Hu

BANTAM BOOKS
NEW YORK · TORONTO · LONDON · SYDNEY · AUCKLAND

A NOTE TO READERS: Although there were Egyptian pharaohs named Ramses, Ramses the Thirteenth was not a real pharaoh.

To Billy Carmen

RL 2, 005-008

A CURSE ON ELIZABETH
A Bantam Book / July 1995

Sweet Valley High® and Sweet Valley Kids are trademarks of Francine Pascal

Conceived by Francine Pascal

Produced by Daniel Weiss Associates, Inc.
33 West 17th Street
New York, NY 10011

Cover art by Susan Tang

ISBN: 0-553-48284-X

Published simultaneously in the United States and Canada

Bantam Books are published by Bantam Books, a division of Bantam Doubleday Dell Publishing Group, Inc. Its trademark, consisting of the words "Bantam Books" and the portrayal of a rooster, is registered in the U.S. Patent and Trademark Office and in other countries. Marca Registrada. Bantam Books, 1540 Broadway, New York, New York 10036.

PRINTED IN THE UNITED STATES OF AMERICA

0 9 8 7 6 5 4 3 2 1

Maybe that's also why Jessica doesn't believe that something mysterious happened at the museum. Something mysterious, and very, very scary.

But the story doesn't begin at the museum. Or the library. It all started on an ordinary day in Mrs. Otis's classroom. . . .

"A coffin?" I whispered. "How creepy."

"I think it's cool," Jessica whispered back. "It must be the fanciest coffin in the whole world."

Andy Franklin turned around. "Shh!" he said.

"Sorry," I whispered.

Our class was sitting in a semicircle in the front of the classroom. We were watching a video about the tomb of King Ramses the Thirteenth. He was a king in ancient Egypt—that's a country far from the United States.

3

King Ramses lived more than three thousand years ago. Back then, kings were called pharaohs. King Ramses' tomb wasn't discovered until last year. That's a long time to be hidden! An exhibit of the beautiful things from his tomb was touring the United States. Mrs. Otis was taking our class to see it at the Los Angeles History Museum.

Jessica and I watched the rest of the video without whispering.

"I can't wait to get to the museum," Jessica said as we took our seats.

"Me neither," I said.

"I want to see the jewelry," Lila Fowler said. The pharaoh had been buried with mounds of jewelry. One necklace was especially pretty. It was made from colorful stones and gold.

"I think the burial masks sound neat," Amy Sutton said.

"And we have to check out that coffin," Jessica added.

"I want to see the mummy," Andy said.

"Me, too!" Lila said.

Jessica and Amy nodded.

I looked at my friends in surprise. I thought they were crazy.

Do you know what a mummy is? Well, I'll tell you. It is a dead body that has been wrapped up in lots and lots of bandages and tar. The ancient Egyptians were very good at making mummies. Some of their mummies lasted thousands of years. King Ramses' mummy was in such good shape that it traveled all the way from Egypt to Sweet Valley! Pretty gross, huh?

"Yuck!" I said. "Mummies are too creepy for me."

Later that morning, a college student

5

came to talk to our class. He worked at the Museum. He had been there when King Ramses' tomb was discovered.

"This is Henry," Mrs. Otis announced. "He has a lot of interesting things to tell you."

"Hello, everyone," Henry said.

"Henry's hair is funny," Jessica whispered. "It's so messy."

Lila giggled. "It sticks straight up."

Henry told us about the pyramids. The pyramids are big buildings made of stone blocks. The ancient Egyptians built them on top of pharaohs' tombs. A few queens had pyramids, too.

The pyramids are a neat shape. They are square at the bottom. All four sides are triangles. The triangles meet in a point at the top. Also, the pyramids are huge. Henry told us that King Ramses the Thirteenth had been buried under two *million* blocks of stone.

"The ancient Egyptians built King Ramses' pyramid long before he died," Henry explained. "That means they had to have a way to get the king's body inside the tomb—*after* the pyramid was finished. There had to be a tunnel running from outside the pyramid to inside the tomb. Even though we knew that, it still took us a long time to find the opening. It was very well hidden. The ancient Egyptians made sure King Ramses would be safe."

Jessica must have still been thinking about the mummy. "Maybe they wanted to be sure we'd be safe from *him*," she whispered.

I giggled.

"Do you have any questions?" Henry asked.

7

"How much is the coffin worth?" Jessica called out.

"It is priceless," Henry said. "So are most of the items uncovered in the tomb."

"Aren't you worried someone might steal them?" Lila asked.

"Yes," Henry said. "That's why the museum has hired many extra guards. We also have an excellent alarm system. Only a superthief could steal anything from the museum."

Eva Simpson raised her hand. "When you opened the tomb, weren't you afraid the mummy would get you?"

"*I* wasn't. But it—" Henry suddenly put his hand on his head. He slowly closed and opened his eyes. "Um, it was hard to get Egyptians to work for us."

"Why?" Mrs. Otis asked.

"Superstition," Henry said. "I—I'm

8

sorry. But that will have to be the last question. I'm not feeling very well. Thank you for having me." Without any more explanation, Henry left the room.

Mrs. Otis looked surprised.

I raised my hand. "May I use the dictionary?"

"Sure," Mrs. Otis said.

I got up and hurried over to the class dictionary. I sounded out "superstition" and looked it up. When I found the word, I was surprised. I thought "superstition" would mean "busy" or something like that. But this is what the dictionary said: "A belief based on fear. For example, the belief that a black cat will bring bad luck is a superstition." I wondered what the Egyptians were afraid of. Could it have been the mummy?

"OK, everyone, listen up," Mrs. Otis called.

I ran back to my seat.

"I want all of you to do a report on the Egyptian pyramids," Mrs. Otis told us. "You will work in pairs—I'll assign partners."

Jessica crossed her fingers for luck. She hopes it will keep her from having to work with a boy. She hates boys. I don't cross my fingers. I don't mind working with boys.

Mrs. Otis started to read from a list.

Jessica got to work with Lila, who is one of her best friends. She was happy.

I was going to work with Andy. I was happy too. Andy is very smart. I knew we could do a good report together.

"Please sit with your partners," Mrs. Otis said. "I want you to choose the subject of your report."

I moved next to Andy.

"I just found out something interesting," I said.

"What?" Andy asked.

I told Andy what "superstition" meant.

He smiled. "Let's do our report on pyramids and superstitions."

"Good idea!" I said.

But when we told Mrs. Otis our idea, she looked worried. "You might not find any information on superstitions at the museum," she said. "You'll have to do some extra work."

"That's OK with me," I said.

"Me, too," Andy agreed.

"You should be able to find the information you need at the library," Mrs. Otis said.

"Goody!" I said. "I love going to the library."

When we went back to our seats, I

told Jessica about the subject Andy and I had chosen.

"Lila and I picked a good subject too," Jessica said. "We're going to do our report on the coffin."

"That's creepy," I said.

"I know," Jessica said with a smile.

CHAPTER 2

King Tut's Lesson

"The pharaoh's tomb is cursed," Andy announced.

I nodded. "Anyone who interrupts the mummy's sleep dies."

It was two days later. Our class was on a bus heading for the Los Angeles History Museum. I was sitting with Andy. Lila and Jessica were in the seat in front of us. Todd and Winston were behind us. Amy and Eva were across the aisle.

Andy and I had spent the evening before at the library. Mrs. Franklin, Andy's mother, had helped us find books about ancient Egypt. Some of those books were pretty scary! Especially the old, dusty one about the Curse of the Pharaohs. That book was so good that I checked it out of the library. I read most of it after dinner. Boy, did I have a hard time sleeping!

"Remember how Henry said they couldn't get Egyptians to work on the dig?" I asked.

The other kids all nodded.

"Well, that was because they were afraid they'd die!" Andy said. Behind his glasses, his eyes were round.

Eva shook her head. "You guys are crazy."

"It *does* sound silly," Todd agreed.

"Do you believe in ghosts too?" Winston asked in a teasing voice.

"We are not making this up," I said.

I had already told Jessica all about the curse. "I didn't believe it at first, either,"

she told the others. "But Elizabeth showed me the book. It was from the *library*."

"Have you guys ever heard of King Tut?" Andy asked.

"I haven't," Amy said.

"He was an Egyptian pharaoh," Andy said. "Just like Ramses the Thirteenth. He was only two years older than us when he became king."

"Wow," Jessica said. "I'd like to become queen in two years."

"Me, too," Lila said.

"King Tut's tomb was discovered back in 1922," I told them. "A man named Lord Carnarvon was the first to open it."

"Lord?" Amy repeated.

"Yeah," I said. "He was from England. Anyway, two months after discovering the tomb, Lord Carnarvon died. The night he died, all of the lights in Cairo—that's a big city in Egypt—went out."

"That doesn't prove anything," Amy pointed out. "Maybe he was really, really old."

"That's not all," Andy told her. "Two dozen men who helped with the dig also died soon after."

"Really?" Winston looked a little worried.

"Really," I said.

"Do you know what I think?" Jessica asked.

"What?" Amy whispered.

"I think Henry is cursed," Jessica said. "He was there when they opened King Ramses' tomb. And then he got sick and had to leave our class."

"That's true," Andy said.

I was starting to feel a little afraid. I hoped King Ramses the Thirteenth wouldn't be angry with us for going to the museum. But what if he *was*?

PUFPHHH! Just then there was a loud explosion outside the bus!

Andy gasped.

The bus lurched to one side. It started to shake.

"What's happening?" Jessica cried out.

The driver pulled the bus over to the side of the road.

Mrs. Otis was talking to him in a low voice. When the bus stopped, she stood up and faced us. "Don't worry, kids," she said. "Everything is fine."

"What was that noise?" Lila sounded worried.

"That's what I'm going to find out," the bus driver said. He got off the bus. Mrs. Otis followed him.

I went over to Eva and Amy's seat. We all tried to look out the window.

But we couldn't tell what was going on. It was a rainy day. All we could see was the top of Mrs. Otis's umbrella.

I sat back down next to Andy.

"This is very odd," he whispered to me.

"What?"

Andy looked scared. "Something happened to the bus at the exact moment we were talking about the Curse of the Pharaohs."

"Cut it out," I told Andy. "You're giving me the creeps."

"Sorry," Andy said.

Mrs. Otis climbed back onto the bus.

"What happened?" Caroline Pearce asked.

"We have a flat tire," Mrs. Otis said. "It will take a while to fix."

"What rotten luck," Jessica said.

I didn't think luck had anything to do with it.

CHAPTER 3

Sharp Teeth

Changing the tire took a long time. We got bored waiting on the bus. Finally we started moving again. But by then, half an hour had gone by. When the bus pulled up in front of the museum at last, we all cheered.

"Look at this place," Jessica said.

I skipped down the steps of the bus. "Wow! It's so fancy!"

Long ago, the museum must have been someone's house. It was an old stone mansion, with only a few windows.

"Everyone over here, please!" Mrs. Otis called. "Let's get organized. We have a lot to see before lunch."

We all crowded around Mrs. Otis. She counted to make sure we were all there. "Remember the buddy system," Mrs. Otis told us. "Everyone stay with your partner—the same person you are working on your report with."

Andy smiled at me. "You're my buddy."

I nodded. "And you're mine." Andy, Jessica, Lila, and I walked through a set of huge wood-and-iron doors. We passed through a pretty entry room. And *then* we had to walk through another set of doors to get into the museum.

"Look at the fancy light!" Lila cried. A big crystal chandelier was hanging over our heads.

"Check out the armor," Andy said.

"Neat!" Todd Wilkins said.

The front hall of the museum was lined with metal suits of armor. A big sword stood next to each one.

Jessica wrinkled her nose. "I don't like this stuff. It's scary."

"The museum looks like a haunted castle," Lila added.

Mrs. Otis hurried us up the stairs. We went through an exhibit about the earth in prehistoric times. It was interesting, but I kept thinking about the pharaoh's tomb. That's what I really wanted to see.

But then Andy gasped. "Look at that!"

"Wow!" Jessica cried. "What is that?"

"It looks like an elephant," Andy said.

"It's too big to be an elephant," I argued.

"And it's furrier than an elephant," Lila said.

"And much, much meaner," Jessica added.

Andy nodded. "Look at those tusks!"

We were all staring at a life-size model of a gigantic animal. Its tusks—the long, pointed teeth that stuck out of each side of its mouth—were huge and gleaming.

Mrs. Otis came up behind us. "That's a woolly mammoth," she said. "Kind of scary, isn't it?"

"Definitely," Lila said.

"Well, don't worry," Mrs. Otis said. "The last mammoths on earth died out about ten thousand years ago."

Jessica laughed. "That's good. Because I wouldn't want to have one of those after me."

CHAPTER 4

Oops!

Soon it was time for us to see the Egyptian stuff. The exhibit was in a special section of the museum. We took an elevator to get there. There were mobs of people in line. Finally the guard let us inside.

"We're in!" I exclaimed.

"Hurray!" Jessica yelled.

A young woman came up to our group. She had a blond ponytail and she wore a red jacket. "Welcome to the treasures of King Ramses the Thirteenth!" she greeted us. "I'm Peggy, your guide. Please follow me."

Peggy told us how the Egyptians farmed. She talked about the Nile—that's a big river in Egypt. Lots of kids asked questions. But I was too excited to ask anything. I wanted Peggy to tell us about the snakes.

The snakes were everywhere! There were big aquariums set into the wall all the way around the room. Each one had a tiny bright-red sticker on it. I went over to get a closer look at the aquariums, and I could see that the stickers all read: POISONOUS. I was very curious. What did poisonous snakes have to do with life in ancient Egypt?

I asked Peggy.

"The ancient Egyptians had many gods," she explained. "At the time King Ramses lived, the most powerful god of all was Ra. He was the sun god.

In ancient Egyptian art, Ra is represented by a cobra. That's the kind of snake you see in this room. Cobras were very important in Egypt. That's why we have so many in the exhibit."

"Can they get out?" Caroline Pearce asked nervously.

"Don't worry," Peggy said. "The glass is nice and thick."

Andy put his face right next to one of the aquariums. "I wish I could see them closer."

"Closer?" I repeated.

"Sure," Andy said. "I love snakes."

"Even poisonous ones?" I asked.

"Especially poisonous ones," Andy said.

I'm not afraid of most snakes. Once I even held a boa constrictor. But boa constrictors are not poisonous. I wasn't sure I liked the idea of snakes that wanted to *poison* me.

I imagined the cobras getting out. Slithering across the floor. Climbing up my legs . . . Yuck! Andy was crazy. I didn't want to get any closer to them.

"Let's go," Peggy called out. She led us into the next room. There was nothing but a sign and an elevator door. Peggy stopped next to the sign. It read CAPSTONE. When we had all gathered around, she asked "Does anyone know what a capstone is?"

I didn't.

But Andy raised his hand.

Peggy called on him.

"It's the stone at the tippy-top of a pyramid," Andy said. "It's shaped like a pyramid, too."

"That's right," Peggy said.

I told you Andy was smart.

"I want you to imagine that we are all floating way up in the air," Peggy said. "We're level with the capstone of King Ramses' pyramid." Peggy gave us a moment to imagine it. Then she stepped forward and pushed a button.

The elevator doors opened. Once we were all inside, Peggy pushed another button. We started to go down . . . down . . . down. . . . Finally the elevator stopped.

"We have just come down one hundred and twenty-five feet," Peggy told us. "It seemed like a long way, didn't it?"

"Yeah!" everyone shouted at once.

Peggy winked at us. "The distance we just traveled was exactly *one quarter* of the way from the capstone of King Ramses' pyramid down to his tomb."

"Wow," Jessica whispered to me. "Pyramids sure are tall."

"Why didn't you make it so we came down the real distance?" I asked.

Peggy laughed. "We would have had to dig a really deep hole for that!" She pushed another button, and the elevator doors opened. We all rushed out of the elevator. We were standing in a model of King Ramses' tomb. Just in front of us was the coffin we had seen in the video. But now there was a velvet rope in front of it. There was also a museum guard standing nearby. Lots of people were looking at the coffin.

Jessica stood on tiptoe to see better. "It's even fancier in real life!"

"It's beautiful," I said. But at the same time, a shiver ran up my spine. It *was* beautiful, but it was still a *coffin*.

"Hey, there's the mummy!" Andy yelled.

"Line up!" Mrs. Otis called. Andy frowned. He wanted to look at the mummy.

Peggy led us to the other side of the room. We looked at vases and necklaces and masks. Jessica and I were amazed.

"Egyptian kings sure were buried with a lot of loot!" Jessica said.

Finally we got to the coffin. We looked at it closely. There were tiny paintings all over it. They showed the pharaoh hunting from a chariot. The chariot was pulled by a horse. Animals raced away from the pharaoh as he raised his spear at them.

"Keep moving!" Peggy called.

I groaned.

"Let's give everyone a chance to see," Mrs. Otis said.

"Come on," Jessica said. She pulled me toward the mummy, which was lying in a mummy case.

Andy and Lila were right behind us.

"He's so gross!" Andy sounded happy.

31

Jessica, Andy, Lila, and I examined the mummy for a long time. It was hard to believe there was actually a body underneath all that material. Thinking about it gave me the creeps.

Charlie Cashman and Jim Sturbridge were behind us in line. They were trying to see the mummy.

"Hurry up," Jim told us.

"We're getting information for our project," Lila said.

"I don't care," Jim yelled. "I want to see the mummy."

Jessica didn't pay any attention to Jim. She leaned toward the pharaoh for a better look. Charlie sneaked up behind her. Before I could stop him, he gave Jessica a shove. Jessica fell against the mummy case. And the lights went out.

The room was plunged into darkness.

CHAPTER 5

Escape!

The pharaoh's tomb echoed with shouts. It sounded as if everyone was screaming and yelling at once.

"What happened?" Lila asked.

"The lights went out," Andy told her calmly. "You know what this reminds me of? The night Lord Carnarvon died."

Lila groaned.

"I can't see a thing." Jessica sounded panicky.

I was scared too. "Me neither," I said.

"It's OK," Mrs. Otis called out. "Everything is going to be fine. I want all of you to sit down right where you are."

Jessica slipped her hand into mine. We sank down to the floor. We scooted as far away from the mummy case as possible.

Suddenly there was a crash of thunder from outside. Jessica squeezed my hand tighter. The tomb was very dark. The only light came from two exit signs. I looked around the tomb. It looked different in the darkness. Spookier. The jewels in the necklaces were shining—even though no light was hitting them. For a second, I thought I saw the mummy's finger wiggle. But I told myself I was imagining things.

"I wonder why the lights went out," I whispered to Jessica.

"It's because I bumped into the mummy case." Jessica still sounded scared. "King Ramses the Thirteenth is mad at me."

"That can't be it," I told Jessica. But a shiver shot up my spine. Maybe Jessica was right. What if the museum was cursed by the pharaohs?

"Mrs. Otis," I called. "Why can't we leave?"

"We'll go soon," Mrs. Otis said. "Just as soon as Peggy comes back. She's getting a light."

After what felt like forever, Peggy appeared. She was holding a huge flashlight.

"OK, kids," Peggy said. "I'm going to lead you outside. Stay close together and hold hands. Let's go!"

Jessica and I helped each other up. We held hands as we followed Peggy down a long, dark hallway. Lila was holding Jessica's other hand. Peggy led our class through a back door. We came out into a garden behind the museum. It was raining. From outside, we could see that the entire museum was dark.

"Boy, am I glad to be out of there," Jessica said.

"Me, too," I replied.

"Me, three," Lila added.

"OK, kids, follow me!" Mrs. Otis called. Walking quickly, she led us around the side of the museum. Our bus was waiting in the parking lot. We all wanted to get out of the rain, so we ran toward the bus. Mrs. Otis told us to stop, but no one listened.

When we were almost to the bus, Caroline Pearce slipped in the mud and fell. She started to cry.

Mrs. Otis hurried over to her. "Caroline! Are you all right?"

I started toward Caroline. What if she was hurt? But Jessica grabbed my hand. "Come on," she said. "Mrs. Otis is taking care of her."

Lila, Jessica, and I rushed onto the bus. Lila and Jessica slipped into their seat. I looked around for Andy. He wasn't in our seat. I didn't see him anywhere!

"Oh, no! Andy is gone," I whispered to Jessica and Lila.

Jessica's eyes were wide. "Where did he go?"

"I don't know," I said. "I haven't seen him since we were in the tomb."

"Do you think he's still in there?" Jessica asked.

I nodded.

"Maybe the mummy got him," Lila suggested.

I took a deep breath. "I have to go find him."

"Why?" Lila asked.

"Because he's my buddy," I said. "I was supposed to stay with him. If I were lost, Andy would look for me."

"You can't go back in there alone," Jessica said. "I'm coming with you."

"Thanks," I said.

Jessica turned to Lila. "You should come too. You're my buddy, and we're supposed to stick together."

Lila crossed her arms over her chest. "There's no way I'm going back in there! That place is cursed."

"Fine," Jessica said. "Be that way."

Lila frowned, but she didn't get up.

Jessica and I hurried off the bus.

Mrs. Otis was still outside. She was helping Caroline brush the mud off her white tights.

"I can't let Mrs. Otis know I forgot my buddy," I whispered. Jessica and I sneaked around to the other side of the bus. Then we ran toward the museum.

CHAPTER 6

Crash!

Jessica and I ran straight to the museum's main entrance. But as we got closer to the door, we slowed down. All of the lights in the museum were still out. It was hard to walk back into that horrible darkness.

"Come on," Jessica said. "We'll go in together."

"OK."

We joined hands. Slowly, hesitantly, we tiptoed inside. In the main hallway, the swords and suits of armor were gleaming dimly. Not only was it dark, but the building was nearly deserted. Only a few voices echoed from somewhere far away.

"Where should we look?" Jessica was whispering, but her voice sounded loud.

"In the Egyptian exhibit," I whispered back.

We tiptoed down the hall.

"Andy?" I wanted to yell, but my voice came out a whisper.

"Andy," Jessica called softly. "Where are you?"

BOOM!

Jessica and I both screamed.

"It—it's OK," Jessica whispered. "It's only thunder."

My hands were shaking. "Let's find Andy quick and get out of here."

The thunder was still rumbling.

"Deal," Jessica said.

The thunder died away as we hurried

down the hall. Suddenly, Jessica stopped me.

"What's that sound?" she whispered.

I stood still and listened. I could feel my heart pounding. "I don't know," I finally said. "But it's coming from somewhere ahead of us."

"Doesn't it sound like a growl?" Jessica asked.

I listened again. Jessica was right. It *did* sound like a growl.

"Let's get out of here!" I yelled.

Jessica and I turned and ran back the way we had come.

I ran as fast as I could toward the dim spot of light shining through the main entrance. About halfway there, I turned around to see if someone—or some*thing*—was after us.

Nothing was. Yet.

"Watch out!" Jessica yelled.

I spun around. A suit of armor was right in front of me. I tried to stop, but it was too late. I hit the suit of armor full force. It crashed down on me.

I fell to the floor. Everything went black.

CHAPTER 7

Hunted

When I opened my eyes, Jessica was kneeling beside me. "Hurry! Get up!" she yelled. "It's coming closer!"

I still felt woozy. But the terror in Jessica's voice made me sit up.

"Come on," Jessica said as she pulled me to my feet. "It's not much farther. We're almost to the main door."

I tried to walk, but I was too dizzy. "Hang on a minute," I said.

"There isn't time!" Jessica dragged me the last few steps to the door. I tried to walk, but I kept stumbling.

"Oh, no," Jessica said when we got to the door. "This can't be happening!"

I could feel a huge bump on my head. I reached up to rub it. "What's the matter?" I muttered.

"The door!" Jessica cried. "It's locked!"

"What?" I said. "It was wide open a minute ago."

Jessica threw herself against the door and started pounding on it. "Let us out! Please, let us out!"

"Calm down," I told Jessica. My head was starting to clear. But I was getting a booming headache. Jessica's yelling hurt my ears.

"I can't calm down!" Jessica moaned. "It's coming closer. It's going to get us."

I listened. Jessica was right. The sound *was* much closer. I could still

hear the growling. But now there was another sound, too. Something that sounded like footsteps. I pushed Jessica aside and started to bang on the thick wooden door myself.

"Help!" I yelled.

"Please let us out!" Jessica added.

Nobody came. The sound was getting closer. The growl was getting louder.

Suddenly, Jessica stopped pounding. She slid down to the floor and put her head in her hands.

"What are you doing?" I asked. "Help me!"

"We're doomed!" Jessica said. "The ghost of King Ramses the Thirteenth is after us. We can't get away."

"Don't say that," I said. "Somebody must have thought the museum was empty. That's why this door is locked."

"No," Jessica said. "We're locked in

here because I bumped into the mummy case. The pharaoh's going to get us. And it's all my fault!"

"That's silly," I said.

"You said it yourself," Jessica insisted. "Anyone who disturbs the mummy's sleep dies."

"Those footsteps are probably a guard," I said. At the same time, I noticed they were getting even closer.

"You're just trying to make me feel better," Jessica said.

"Look, I'll prove it," I said. Before Jessica could stop me, I stepped out into the hallway.

And then I screamed.

CHAPTER 8

The Mammoth Lives

"What's wrong?" Jessica asked. "What did you see?"

"I saw Andy," I told her. "He almost ran me down."

Andy burst into the entranceway. When he saw the door was locked, he looked as if he were going to cry.

I realized the footsteps had stopped. They must have been Andy's all along. Relief flooded through me.

Jessica stopped looking worried and started looking mad. "Where have you been?" she asked Andy in an angry voice.

"Never mind," Andy panted. "We have to go. It's coming!"

"What's coming?" I asked.

Andy shook his head. "You don't want to know. But trust me. We can't stay here. Follow me."

Andy ran back out into the main hallway. Jessica and I traded looks. Then we ran after Andy.

Once we were out of the entranceway, I glanced behind me—quickly. I didn't want to run into any more suits of armor! But this time I saw what was after us.

It was the woolly mammoth!

He didn't look stuffed anymore. He was growling, licking his chops, and running. Fast. His tusks looked sharp.

I turned around and started to run faster.

I am usually a good runner. I'm a star on my soccer team. But I couldn't

run fast. My left ankle was starting to hurt. I must have hit my foot when I crashed into the suit of armor. Jessica and Andy were way ahead of me. The woolly mammoth was closing in.

I couldn't catch up to the others.

Jessica stopped running and turned around. "Lizzie, hurry!" she yelled.

"Keep going!" I called to Jessica.

She started to run again.

I glanced back.

The woolly mammoth was only a few steps behind me.

I tried to run faster, but I couldn't. I looked up ahead. Andy and Jessica had disappeared.

I kept stumbling forward. I could feel the woolly mammoth's hot breath on my neck. It smelled awful. I braced myself for the bite of his tusks.

CHAPTER 9

Out of Breath

Someone reached out and yanked me to the side. I found myself watching the woolly mammoth charge past. "What happened?" I gasped.

"It's OK," Andy said. "We pulled you in."

In? I looked around and saw that we were in the elevator.

Andy peeked out. "He's turning around! He's coming this way!"

Quickly, Jessica pushed the DOOR CLOSE button. There was a long pause. Then the elevator doors slid shut. We could hear the woolly mammoth's tusks scratching against the metal.

"Go, go," Jessica whispered.

The elevator started to move.

"Yes!" Jessica shouted.

Andy and I sighed with relief. The woolly mammoth wouldn't be able to follow us down in the elevator.

"Are you all right?" Jessica asked me.

"I think so," I said. "I couldn't run any faster because I hurt my foot. Thanks for grabbing me."

Jessica smiled. "No problem. I would never let my twin sister be a woolly mammoth's lunch."

I laughed.

The elevator stopped.

"What's the matter?" Jessica asked. "Why aren't the doors opening?"

"When we were in here before, Peggy had to push a button to open the doors," I said. "Remember?"

"That's right," Andy said. He searched for the button and pushed it. The elevator doors opened. We walked out into the pharaoh's tomb.

"What do we do now?" Jessica asked.

Andy shrugged. "I don't even know what's going on."

"Well, one thing is for sure," Jessica said. "Whatever is happening, it's pretty weird."

"And powerful," I added. "I mean, stuffed animals don't usually just come to life."

"Do you think it's the Curse of the Pharaohs?" Andy asked.

"Yes," Jessica said.

I nodded.

"So we're doomed, right?" Jessica asked. "You can't exactly fight a curse."

"I think—we should—stay here,"

Andy suggested. He put his hands on his knees and took a deep breath.

"Andy, is something wrong?" I asked.

He shook his head. "I'm just—out of breath—from running."

"I don't think that's it," I said. "I'm having a hard time breathing too."

"So am I," Jessica said. "It's like there isn't enough—air in here."

Suddenly lights began to flash. A loud alarm went off.

CHAPTER 10

Trapped in the Tomb

WA! WA! WAHH, WAHH, WAHH! the alarm wailed.

"What's going on?" I yelled. It was hard to scream over the alarm. Especially since I was so out of breath.

"We—have—to—find—the—alarm!" Andy said. He hurried toward the blinking lights. Jessica and I were right behind him.

"Here—it—is," Jessica gasped.

Andy and I gathered around her.

"It's—for—the—air—system—in the tomb," Andy said. "The—alarm must—mean—the system has failed."

"What does that mean?" Jessica asked.

"No air," Andy said. "We have to—get out."

"The—elevator," I said.

We all stumbled over to the elevator and got in. I pushed the DOOR CLOSE button. The doors slid shut. I pushed the CAPSTONE button. Nothing happened. The elevator didn't move.

"Push the button!" Jessica cried.

"I did," I told her. I pushed the button again and again. Still, nothing happened.

"Someone will—hear the alarm," Andy gasped. "We'll be—rescued in no time. Just—have to wait."

"We—should not talk," I said. "It takes too much air."

Andy and Jessica nodded.

I leaned against the elevator door. I counted to one hundred. Nobody came. I felt very sleepy. I closed my eyes. I could feel myself falling asleep. . . .

Andy shook me awake. "We have to—find another way out. We can't stay here any longer."

I shuddered. Andy was right. If I had fallen asleep, I never would have gotten out of the tomb. "Let's go!" I agreed. I didn't want to spend the rest of my life with the mummy!

Jessica pushed the DOOR OPEN button. We went back out into the pharaoh's tomb. The alarm was still ringing. Andy and I waited while Jessica walked around the room. She found a door, but it was locked. Jessica kept looking. Finally, she motioned for us to come over to her. She was yelling something, but I couldn't hear her over the alarm.

Andy and I ran to Jessica. She had found a tiny winding staircase running up the side of the elevator. Jessica motioned for us to climb up. Andy put his foot on the first step and started to climb.

Jessica went next.

I followed. Climbing the stairs was difficult with no air. I felt very sleepy and faint.

"How are you guys doing?" Andy called down.

"OK, I guess," Jessica yelled back.

I didn't feel OK. My lungs were on fire. I was tired and sweaty. And the air didn't seem to be getting any better.

Andy smiled at us. "Don't give up. You're almost there!"

Suddenly I saw something flash past my eyes. A few seconds later, I heard it hit on the stone floor. I looked down.

The floor was far, far away. We had been climbing for a long time. I remembered Peggy had said the elevator went down over a hundred feet.

"Oops," Andy said.

"What was that?" Jessica asked.

"My glasses," Andy told her.

"Oh, no," I said weakly.

"Forget them!" Andy yelled. "Just keep climbing. The air is much better up here."

I forced myself to forget about the glasses. I had to think about climbing. The air was better just a little farther up. But could I make it that far?

CHAPTER 11

Cobras on the Loose

I barely managed to keep climbing the stairs. I had to stop and rest twice. But as I got up higher, my head felt clearer and my legs felt stronger. By the time I reached the top, I felt almost normal. I took deep breaths of the fresh air.

There was a door at the top of the stairs. I opened it and walked out onto the main floor of the museum. Andy and Jessica were waiting for me.

"I've never been so happy to breathe before!" I exclaimed. "That was close."

"Too close," Jessica agreed.

Andy didn't say anything. He looked scared.

"What's wrong?" I asked him.

"Well . . ." Andy said. "Do you think the woolly mammoth is still around?"

I gulped. I hadn't thought of that. I quickly looked up and down the hall. "Well, it's not close by," I said.

"How do you know?" Andy asked.

"Because she can't see him," Jessica said.

Andy squinted his eyes. He looked down the hall. "Are you sure?"

"Sure I'm sure," I said. "Andy, what can you see without your glasses?"

"Anything," Andy said. "Just as long as it's right in front of me."

Jessica put her hand about two feet in front of Andy's nose. She held up three fingers. "How many fingers do you see?" she asked.

64

"One?" Andy guessed.

Jessica and I groaned. Without his glasses, Andy was practically blind. He wasn't going to be able to move very fast.

"Let's get out of here before the woolly mammoth comes back," I said.

"We'd better get started *now*," Jessica said.

I nodded. "Come on, Andy. You can hold on to my arm."

"OK," Andy said.

"Do you guys know where are we?" I asked.

"No," Andy said.

Jessica shook her head. "It doesn't matter. We can't go back to the main entrance anyway. That door's locked."

"Right," I said. "We have to find another door—fast! I think you should be our leader," I told Jessica.

Jessica nodded. She started down the hall.

Andy and I followed more slowly. He was holding on to my left arm. I kept him from walking into anything. He let me lean on him. That took the pressure off my bad ankle.

Jessica led us through a doorway and into a room.

"Hey, I know where we are," I said. "This is the 'Life in Ancient Egypt' room."

"I know," Jessica said. She was standing in a doorway on the other side of the room. "I'm going to run ahead and see what I can find."

"Good idea," I said. "Hurry."

Jessica disappeared through the door.

"I'm sorry I'm so slow," Andy said.

"It's OK," I told him. "It's not your fault you dropped your glasses."

"But what if the woolly mammoth comes back?" Andy asked.

"I don't know," I said.

"Elizabeth," Andy said sternly. "I'm serious. If the woolly mammoth comes back, I want you to leave me behind."

"No," I said. "I couldn't."

"Promise you will," Andy said.

"No way."

"Do you promise?" Andy asked again.

I didn't pay any attention to Andy's question. "I think there's something in here," I said. "Do you see it?"

"No," Andy said immediately. "What does it look like?"

"Well . . ." It was hard to describe. There was something on the floor—I could see it out of the corner of my eye. But when I looked straight at it, it squirmed away.

I kept staring down. I caught a

glimpse of another thing on the floor just ahead of us. Again. And again. And again. Whatever the mysterious objects were, there were a lot of them.

The room was pretty dark. It was impossible for me to see what the things were—until one brushed against my leg. It felt smooth and cool. Like a snake!

"Hang on a second," I told Andy. I stopped walking and leaned over. I couldn't believe it. The entire floor was squirming with cobras! They looked much bigger than they had in their aquariums. Each one was about as long as I am tall.

These snakes are poisonous! I thought. *I bet King Ramses the Thirteenth sent them to get revenge on us.*

Jessica appeared in the far doorway.

"Don't come in here!" I hollered at her. "The cobras are out."

Andy gasped. "They are?"

"Yes!" I was starting to feel panicky. "What do we do?"

"Just keep walking," Andy said. "Don't make any sudden movements."

Andy and I inched along so slowly, it took us at least five minutes to get to the exit. As soon as we got into the hallway, Jessica slammed the door.

Andy and I breathed deep sighs of relief.

"Now, *that* was close," Andy said.

"You said it." I leaned back against the closed door. "What a day!"

Jessica grabbed my arm and yanked me away from the door.

"What's wrong?" I asked.

Jessica pointed to the door. She looked horrified.

Slowly, I looked where she was pointing. The cobras were trying to squeeze themselves out into the hallway. Dozens of forked tongues flitted underneath the door.

"What are we going to do?" Jessica whimpered.

"What's happening?" Andy asked. He couldn't see the tiny snake tongues.

"The cobras are trying to get out," Jessica told him.

"Do something!" Andy yelled.

"Like what?" Jessica yelled back.

"I know!" I said. I took off my jacket. I pushed it into the crack under the door.

"Good thinking." Jessica grinned at me. "Now the snakes are stuck inside."

"Yeah," Andy said. "But now we can't go back that way."

Jessica shrugged. "So?"

"What if the only way out is on the other side of that door?" Andy said.

CHAPTER 12

The Mummy Moves

"We can't go back," Jessica said. I looked around. We were in a very short hallway. There were only two doors off it. One led into the room with the cobras.

"What's behind the other door?" I asked.

"Stairs," Jessica said.

Andy and I groaned.

"They go up or down," Jessica said. "I think we should go up."

I nodded.

But Andy shook his head.

"Why not?" Jessica asked. "We just escaped from the tomb. I don't want to go back downstairs again."

"There might not be any air down there," I added.

"I know," Andy said. "But we're on the ground floor now. There can't be any doors to the outside *above* us. It's better to go down. If we're lucky, we'll come out in some other part of the museum."

There was a long pause.

"Andy's right," I finally said. "Let's try going downstairs."

"Oh, all right," Jessica grumbled. She started to lead the way down the stairs. Andy and I followed. We got down about five flights before we heard the noise.

Mmwah . . . Ahh . . . Mmwah . . .

The soft noise was coming from somewhere below us. It sounded just like the groan my brother, Steven, makes when he eats too much dinner.

Jessica spun around. Her eyes were wide. "What's that?"

"It sounds like someone is in pain," Andy said.

"Or it could be the mummy," I suggested.

"Elizabeth!" Jessica exclaimed. "Don't say that!"

I shrugged. "Sorry."

"I think it sounds like a person," Andy said.

"Then let's go," I said. "If it *is* a person, we've got to help them."

"Of course, it could be a trap," Andy said thoughtfully.

Jessica groaned. "So what do you guys want to do?"

"Just in case it's a person, we've got to find out what's making the noise,"

Andy said. "But let's be careful."

Finally we reached the bottom. There was only one door off the staircase. We all looked at it.

"What if this leads back into the tomb," I asked.

"Well, we can't go back into the tomb," Andy said. "There's no air."

"I'm not so sure," Jessica said. "Listen."

I listened. All I could hear was someone—or some*thing*—moaning.

"I don't hear anything but that person," Andy said.

"Exactly!" Jessica said. "There *has* to be air in there. Otherwise, no one would be able to moan."

"Mummies probably don't need air to moan," Andy said.

Jessica frowned. "I'm going in."

"I'll come with you," I said.

"Me, too," Andy said. "I think we should stick together."

Jessica opened the door. It *did* lead to the tomb. We waited. Nothing happened, except that the moaning got louder. We crept inside.

"Oh, no!" Andy exclaimed as the door clicked shut behind us.

"What?" I asked.

"We should've put something in the door so it wouldn't close," Andy said.

I tried the door. "It's locked."

"Great," Andy said.

"Over here!" Jessica called.

Andy and I found Jessica looking down at a young man slumped in front of the coffin. He looked very sick.

I gasped. "It's Henry!"

"The college student who came to our class?" Andy asked.

"Yes," I said.

Jessica knelt down next to Henry. She shook his shoulder.

Henry moaned.

"What's wrong?" Jessica asked him.

"I shouldn't be here," Henry said hoarsely.

"Are you here because of the mummy?" Andy asked.

"Yes," Henry said. "I was trying to steal it. And the coffin. And everything else."

"That's terrible!" I exclaimed. "How could you?"

"I wanted the money," Henry said weakly.

"But you told us it was impossible to steal this stuff," Jessica said.

Henry opened his eyes and stared at Jessica. He looked a bit crazy. "Not impossible—only very difficult. A good thief could pull it off. I had everything carefully planned: I arranged for the museum's security alarm to be turned off; I made the lights go out."

"*You* made the lights go out?" Jessica gasped.

"Yes." Henry closed his eyes again.

"So what went wrong?" Andy asked.

"It happened as soon as I touched the coffin," Henry said. "I got terrible pains in my stomach. They're so bad, I can't move. I—I think I'm dying."

"Come on, Henry," I said. "You have to get up. We've got to get you to a doctor."

"No," Henry said. "It's too late for me. I can't escape the Curse of the Pharaohs. . . . But you all must leave here. Quickly." Henry closed his eyes. His head slumped to one side.

Jessica shook Henry's shoulder. "Wake up!"

Henry didn't answer.

"I think he passed out," Andy said.

"We have to help him," I said.

"But he's a thief!" Andy exploded.

"I know," I said. "But we can't just leave him here."

"I agree with Liz," Jessica said.

"Oh, OK," Andy grumbled. "We'll take him with us. But don't forget, we still haven't found a way out."

"Look!" Jessica exclaimed. "Henry had a flashlight just like Peggy's."

"Where?" I asked.

Jessica pointed to the flashlight. It had rolled under the pharaoh's mummy case.

"That could be a big help," Andy said.

"I'll get it," I said. I crawled underneath the mummy case. I picked up the flashlight. At the same time, I noticed a puddle on the floor. I dipped my finger in it and looked at my finger. It was greenish goo. It sort of glowed in the darkness.

I was surprised. "Do you guys see anything leaking?" I called.

"No," Jessica said.

Just then I saw a fresh drop of goo hit the puddle. I looked up. The green stuff was dripping from the mummy!

I jumped. My head hit the mummy case, and I dropped the flashlight. It crashed onto the floor and shattered. I scooted out from under the case.

"What's wrong?" Andy asked.

"Why did you break the flashlight?" Jessica asked.

I couldn't make my mouth work. I just pointed at the mummy.

Jessica and Andy turned around slowly.

Just in time to see three-thousand-year-old King Ramses the Thirteenth sit up!

CHAPTER 13

Through the Window

The mummy swung his feet out of his case. Slowly, carefully, he stood up. His knees went out from under him. He pitched to one side and almost fell. But then he steadied himself.

Jessica, Andy, and I just stared at him. I was too terrified to move. Henry didn't wake up.

The mummy let out a low growl. He turned toward us.

"I think we'd better go now." Jessica's voice was shaky.

"What about Henry?" I asked.

"Leave him," Jessica said.

"We have to get out of here *now,*" Andy agreed.

"We'll get help for Henry once we're outside," Jessica said.

"Wait," I said. "Where can we go? The door to the stairs is locked."

"Maybe the elevator is working now," Jessica said. "I'll check."

Jessica ran over to the elevator. Andy and I kept an eye on the mummy. He seemed to be watching us, too.

"It doesn't work!" Jessica yelled.

"What do we do?" Andy asked.

The mummy took one step toward us. Andy and I backed up.

"We've got to think!" I said.

The mummy took another step.

"Henry!" Andy exclaimed.

"What about him?" Jessica asked.

"He must have planned a way out of here," Andy said.

"Maybe he has a key to the stairs!" Jessica said.

I inched around behind the mummy and leaned down next to Henry. A key ring was hanging from his belt loop. I slipped the keys off. "There are a lot of them," I said.

"Well, hurry up and try them," Andy said.

I ran over to the door to the stairs. I was trying to go fast, so I kept dropping the keys. Finally, I tried one in the lock. It didn't fit. I tried another. It didn't fit, either.

"Come on, Liz," Jessica said.

I looked over my shoulder. The mummy was moving closer to Andy and Jessica.

As quickly as I could, I tried the rest

of the keys on the ring. "None of them fit!" I felt like crying.

"One of them has to!" Andy insisted.

I took a deep breath and tried to think calmly.

"Liz, what are you doing?" Jessica cried.

"There has to be another door," I said.

Jessica gasped. "There is! Back behind the winding staircase. Remember?"

I did. I ran over to the door, which was painted red. I tried the keys again, and the first one fit. "Got it!" I yelled.

Jessica grabbed Andy's hand. We all ran through the door. We came out in a long hallway.

I slammed the door behind us.

"Lock it," Jessica said.

"There's no lock on this side," I told her.

"We can hold it closed," Andy said.

The mummy was on the other side of the door. He was trying to push it open. He was strong.

"I think we'd better try to outrun him," I said.

Andy and Jessica nodded.

"You guys stick together," Jessica said. "I'll run ahead and look for a door."

"OK," I agreed.

Jessica ran down the hallway.

Andy and I followed as fast as we could.

Right away, the mummy pushed through the door. He clomped down the hallway after us. Luckily, he couldn't move very fast—there were too many strips of material wrapped around his body. His arms were wrapped tight against his sides. His legs were wrapped, too, so he could only take tiny steps.

But Andy and I couldn't run fast, either. I was still limping. And since I was leading Andy, he couldn't go any faster than I could.

"What happened to Jessica?" Andy asked me.

"I don't know," I said. "It sure is taking her a long time to find a door."

"Jessica!" Andy yelled. "Where are you?"

"In here," Jessica called back.

Andy and I hurried toward Jessica's voice. We found her in the last room off the hallway. We rushed up to her.

"Did you find a door?" Andy asked.

"No," Jessica cried.

The mummy stumbled into the doorway.

"We're stuck," Andy said. "He's blocking the only way out."

"What are we going to do?" Jessica said tearfully.

"We'll have to fight the mummy," Andy said. "Maybe we can win. It's three against one."

"No," Jessica cried. "He's too strong."

Frantically, I looked around for some way to escape. The room was filled with steam engines, ancient trains, and early automobiles. An old-fashioned plane was hanging from the ceiling.

The windows in the room were high above my head.

There's no way out, I thought miserably.

The mummy growled. He took a step forward.

"Help!" Jessica screamed. "Someone, please help!"

I noticed a ladder leading up to the plane. *We could get into the plane,* I thought. *Maybe we could reach a window from there.* That didn't seem very likely—the plane was pretty far from the windows. It wasn't a good plan. But it was our only chance.

"You guys!" I yelled. "Over here."

Jessica and Andy ran over. "What?" Jessica asked.

"Climb this ladder," I said. "And get into that plane."

Without any questions, Jessica and Andy started to climb. I followed them. The mummy came after me. But when he tried to climb the ladder, he couldn't get his legs up on it. King Ramses was really mad. He roared and shook the ladder.

Jessica and Andy were in the plane.

"Now what?" Jessica asked.

I was still on the ladder. It was swinging back and forth. "Try to reach the window," I yelled.

Jessica reached out toward the window.

The bottom of the ladder swung loose. The mummy had pulled it away from the wall. I raced up the last few steps and jumped into the plane. Just then the top of the ladder came away from the wall. The mummy shook the ladder in the air. He growled furiously.

"I can't reach the window!" Jessica told me.

"Now what?" Andy asked.

I looked up. The plane was held on to the ceiling with tiny wires. One of the wires in the back was about to break. If it did, we would swing loose and crash into the window.

"Rock the plane," I ordered.

"What?" Jessica said.

"Rock the plane back and forth," I explained. "Like a car in a Ferris wheel."

Jessica, Andy, and I started to rock.

I glanced up at the wires. First one, and then the other, snapped under our weight. The plane swung loose.

"Get down!" I yelled.

We all ducked. Jessica screamed as the plane crashed through the window. We were flying through the air, but I didn't care. We were out of the museum!

I looked over the edge of the plane. We were heading right for a tree! We were going to hit it!

I screamed. And then everything went black.

CHAPTER 14

No Place Like Home

"Elizabeth?" asked Jessica's voice. "Elizabeth, can you hear me?"

I opened my eyes.

Jessica was looking down at me. So was Andy.

"She's awake," Jessica said happily.

"That's a relief," Mrs. Otis said.

Mrs. Otis?

I sat up. "When did you get here?" I asked my teacher.

"I never left," Mrs. Otis said. "Now, I want you to lie back and rest for a few minutes. Everything is going to be fine."

I lay back down. "Where am I?" I asked.

"At the history museum," Jessica said. "Remember?"

"Of course!" I said. "But *where* in the history museum?"

"Right at the front entrance," Jessica said. "Where else?"

I turned my head. Sure enough, there was the museum's main entrance. Through the front door I could see the fancy chandelier inside. It was lit up.

That's funny, I thought. *When did the lights come back on?*

"What happened?" I asked.

"You've got a nasty bump on your head," said a man's voice.

"Of course I have a bump," I said. "We hit a tree."

"A tree?" Jessica repeated.

"She probably dreamed that," the man's voice said.

I lifted my head to see who was talking.

"Henry!" I exclaimed.

"Why are you so surprised?" Henry asked with a smile. "Did you forget I work at the museum?"

"No, it's not that," I said. "It just that . . . Do you feel better?"

Henry looked puzzled. "I had a headache at your school the other day. But I've been fine since then."

"Oh," I said.

What's going on? I thought. Then it came to me. Henry didn't want Mrs. Otis to know he was a thief. I wondered if I should turn him in. I couldn't figure out why Andy and Jessica hadn't done that already.

I turned to look at Andy. "Hey!" I

exclaimed. "You got your glasses back!"

"My glasses?" Andy said. "I never lost my glasses."

"Mrs. Otis," Jessica whispered. "Is Elizabeth OK?"

"Don't worry," Mrs. Otis said. "She's just a little confused."

Confused? I wasn't confused. They were the ones who were confused! They were acting as if nothing had happened!

"Elizabeth, I want you to rest for a minute," Mrs. Otis told me. "Don't talk."

"OK," I whispered. Suddenly, I didn't feel like talking.

I thought about what I had just been told. Henry wasn't sick. Andy didn't lose his glasses. We didn't hit a tree. That could mean only one thing: The Curse of the Pharaohs was all a dream.

We had never been stuck in the tomb. Or attacked by cobras. Or chased by a mummy. Those things had only happened in my imagination. But it had seemed so real. . . .

"Elizabeth," Mrs. Otis said gently, "do you remember how you bumped your head?"

I thought for a second. Jessica had said we didn't hit a tree. How else could I have hurt myself? Suddenly I remembered the suit of armor! All of the really spooky things had happened after that.

"Did I crash into a suit of armor?" I finally asked.

"Yes!" Jessica said.

Mrs. Otis smiled at me. "Do you feel well enough to take the bus back to Sweet Valley?"

"Definitely," I said, sitting up. I

couldn't wait to get away from the museum.

"Then let's go," Mrs. Otis said.

Jessica helped me to my feet.

Henry waved good-bye to us. I felt a little funny letting him go. But all of those terrible things had been a dream. Henry was just a college student.

We got onto the bus.

"Hey, Elizabeth!" someone called.

"Are you all right?" said someone else.

Everyone seemed worried about me.

"I'm fine," I said. And it was true. I actually *felt* fine. A little weird, but fine.

Jessica and I sat together.

Andy sat next to Lila.

"Are you really OK?" Lila asked.

I nodded.

"We were so worried about you," Lila

said. "Jessica came running back onto the bus, screaming. She said you hit your head really hard."

"She did," Jessica said.

"I still don't understand what happened after that," I said.

"You passed out!" Jessica exclaimed. "I was so scared! I thought you were dead or something. I came and got Mrs. Otis."

"When did the lights come back on?" I asked.

"Right after Mrs. Otis and I got back to the museum," Jessica said. "She got Henry to carry you outside."

"Why did they go out in the first place?" I asked.

"Because of the storm," Andy told me. "The electricity was out all over Los Angeles."

"Just like the night Lord Carnarvon died," I said.

Andy wiggled his eyebrows. "Exactly!"

"Hey, where were you?" I asked Andy. "This all started because you were missing!"

"I was on the bus the whole time," Andy said. "Talking to Winston."

"You're kidding," I said.

Andy shook his head.

"Mrs. Otis was pretty mad we ran off," Jessica told me.

"She doesn't seem mad now," I said.

"That's probably because you hurt yourself," Lila told me.

"And because she already gave *me* two speeches," Jessica added. "One for each of us."

I laughed and sat back in my seat. I was beginning to believe I really had imagined the whole thing. But then I sat up with a start.

"Hey, where's my jacket?" I asked.

Jessica looked around. "I don't know," she said. "That's funny. I'm sure you had it on when we went back into the museum to look for Andy."

I was sure too. And I was pretty sure I knew where it was. It was pushed under a door inside the museum. Keeping the cobras in.

"Hey, Andy," I said. "Let's do our report on something other than superstitions."

"Like what?" Andy asked.

"Something that has nothing to do with curses," I told him.

Andy thought for a second. Then his face lit up. "I know! We can do it on how the Egyptians made mummies."

I laughed. "Good idea!"

In the puzzle below, you will find ten things Elizabeth learned about in this book. The words are written forward, backward, and diagonally. How many can you find?

1. EGYPT
2. PYRAMID
3. MAMMOTH
4. MUSEUM
5. MUMMY

6. CAPSTONE
7. PHARAOH
8. RAMSES
9. CURSE
10. COBRA

```
Q  F  H  B  V  A  R  B  O  C
P  Y  R  A  M  I  D  Z  U  L
H  J  G  S  U  U  W  R  I  T
A  C  K  D  M  R  S  X  Y  S
R  A  J  O  M  E  D  E  L  E
A  P  E  G  Y  P  T  B  U  S
O  S  N  B  Q  F  U  R  P  M
H  T  O  M  M  A  M  S  G  A
G  O  Z  B  E  T  Y  J  D  R
P  N  V  L  R  I  W  X  Y  F
Q  E  S  B  J  L  U  K  P  H
```

Help the mummy find his way back to the pyramid!

How much do you remember about Elizabeth's adventure? Answer these trivia questions to find out:

1. The second grade is learning about a pharaoh. His name was King _ _ _◯_ _ .

2. The Egyptians believed that there was a _◯_ _ _ on the pharaoh's tomb.

3. The pharaoh was buried under a triangular-shaped building called a ◯_ _ _ _ _ _ .

4. The pharaoh was king of a nation called _ _ _ _◯.

5. Mrs. _ _ _◯ is Elizabeth and Jessica's teacher.

6. _ _ _ _   _ _ _ _ _ _◯_ is Elizabeth's partner on this project.

7. Elizabeth runs through a hall full of cobras. Cobras are a kind of _ _ _ _◯.

8. The stone at the very top of a pyramid is called a _ _ _ _ _◯_ _ .

9. The college student who talks to the class is named _ _ _◯ .

10. _◯_ _   _ _ _ _ _ _ is Jessica's partner on this project.

11. A _ _ _ _ _ _   _ _ _ _◯_ is a huge, prehistoric animal that looks like an elephant.

12. The big river that runs through Egypt is called the ◯_ _ _ .

Now write the circled letters below. When you unscramble them, you'll find the answer to this question: Why was it hard to get Egyptians to work on the mummy's tomb?

_ _ _ _ _ _ _ _ _ _ _ _ _

Answers

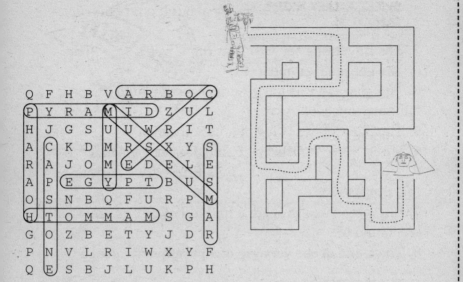

```
Q F H B V A R B O C
P Y R A M I D Z U L
H J G S U U W R I T
A C K D M R S X Y S
R A J O M M E D E L E
A P E G Y P T B U S
O S N B Q F U R P M
H T O M M A M S G A
G O Z B E T Y J D R
P N V L R I W X Y F
Q E S B J L U K P H
```

1. RAMSES
2. CURSE
3. PYRAMID
4. EGYPT
5. OTIS
6. ANDY FRANKLIN
7. SNAKE
8. CAPSTONE
9. HENRY
10. LILA FOWLER
11. WOOLLY MAMMOTH
12. NILE

SUPERSTITION

SIGN UP FOR THE
SWEET VALLEY HIGH®
FAN CLUB!

Hey, girls! Get all the gossip on Sweet
Valley High's® most popular teenagers
when you join our fantastic Fan Club!
As a member, you'll get all of this really
cool stuff:

- Membership Card with your own
  personal Fan Club ID number
- A Sweet Valley High® Secret
  Treasure Box
- Sweet Valley High® Stationery
- Official Fan Club Pencil (for secret
  note writing!)
- Three Bookmarks
- A "Members Only" Door Hanger
- Two Skeins of J. & P. Coats® Embroidery
  Floss with flower barrette instruction
  leaflet
- Two editions of *The Oracle* newsletter
- Plus exclusive Sweet Valley High®
  product offers, special savings,
  contests, and much more!

Be the first to find out what Jessica & Elizabeth Wakefield are up to by joining the
Sweet Valley High® Fan Club for the one-year membership fee of only $6.25 each
for U.S. residents, $8.25 for Canadian residents (U.S. currency). Includes shipping
& handling.

Send a check or money order (do not send cash) made payable to "Sweet Valley
High® Fan Club" along with this form to:

SWEET VALLEY HIGH® FAN CLUB, BOX 3919-B, SCHAUMBURG, IL 60168-3919

NAME_____
(Please print clearly)

ADDRESS_____

CITY_____ STATE _____ ZIP_____
(Required)

AGE _____ BIRTHDAY_____ /_____ /_____

Offer good while supplies last. Allow 6-8 weeks after check clearance for delivery. Addresses without ZIP
codes cannot be honored. Offer good in USA & Canada only. Void where prohibited by law.
©1993 by Francine Pascal   LCI-1383-123